THE MAN WHO CAST NO SHADOW

BY

SEABURY QUINN

British Library Cataloguing-in-Publication Data
A catalogue record for this book is available from
the British Library

Contents

SEABURY QUINN

Seabury Grandin Quinn was born in Washington D.C. in 1889. In 1910, he graduated from law school, and was admitted to the District of Columbia Bar. He served in World War I, and after his Army service became editor of a group of trade papers in New York. His first published work was 'The Law of the Movies' (1917), in *The Motion Picture Magazine*, and his first published fictional story was 'Demons of the Night' (1918), in *Detective Story Magazine*. He introduced the occult detective Jules de Grandin as a character in 1925, and continued writing tales about him until 1951. Quinn's stories were incredibly popular, and between the twenties and fifties he appeared in *Weird Tales* magazine more times than both Robert E. Howard and H. P. Lovecraft. His novel *Roads* was also widely read. Quinn died in old age on Christmas Eve.

'**B**ut no, my friend,' Jules de Grandin shook his sleek, blond head decidedly and grinned across the breakfast table at me, 'we will go to this so kind Madame Norman's tea, of a certainty. Yes.'

'But hang it all,' I replied, giving Mrs Norman's note an irritable shove with my coffee spoon, 'I don't want to go to a confounded tea party! I'm too old and too sensible to dress up in a tall hat and a long coat and listen to the vaporings of a flock of silly flappers. I—'

'*Mordieu*, hear the savage!' de Grandin chuckled delightedly. 'Always does he find excuses for not giving pleasure to others, and always does he frame those excuses to make him more important in his own eyes. Enough of this, Friend Trowbridge; let us go to the kind Madame Norman's party. Always there is something of interest to be seen if one but knows where to look for it.'

'H'm, maybe,' I replied grudgingly, 'but you've better sight than I think you have if you can find anything worth seeing at an afternoon reception.'

The reception was in full blast when we arrived at the Norman mansion in Tuscarora Avenue that afternoon in 192–. The air was heavy with the commingled odors of half a hundred different perfumes and the scent of hot-poured jasmine tea, while the clatter of cup on saucer, laughter, and buzzing conversation filled the wide hall and dining room. In the long double parlors the rugs had been rolled back and young men in frock coats glided over the polished parquetry in company with girls in provocatively short skirts to the belching melody of a saxophone and the drumming rhythm of a piano.

'*Pardieu*,' de Grandin murmured as he viewed the dancers a moment, 'your American youth take their pleasures with seriousness, Friend Trowbridge. Behold their faces. Never a smile, never a laugh. They might be recruits

SEABURY QUINN

3

on their first parade for all the joy they show – ah!' He broke off abruptly, gazing with startled, almost horrified, eyes after a couple whirling in the mazes of a foxtrot at the farther end of the room. '*Nom d'un fromage*,' he murmured softly to himself, 'this matter will bear investigating, I think!'

'Eh, what's that?' I asked, piloting him toward our hostess.

'Nothing; nothing, I do assure you,' he answered as we greeted Mrs Norman and passed toward the dining-room. But I noticed his round, blue eyes strayed more than once toward the parlors as we drank our tea and exchanged amiable nothings with a pair of elderly ladies.

'Pardon,' de Grandin bowed stiffly from the hips to his conversational partner and turned toward the rear drawing room, 'there is a gentleman here I desire to meet, if you do not mind – that tall, distinguished one, with the young girl in pink.'

'Oh, I guess you mean Count Czerny,' a young man laden with an ice in one hand and a glass of non-Volstead punch in the other paused on his way from the dining-room. 'He's a rare bird, all right. I knew him back in '13 when the Balkan Allies were polishing off the Turks. Queer-lookin' duck, ain't he? First-class fightin' man, though. Why, I saw him lead a bayonet charge right into the Turkish lines one day, and when he'd shot his pistol empty he went at the enemy with his teeth! Yes, sir, he grabbed a Turk with both hands and bit his throat out, hanged if he didn't.'

'Czerny,' de Grandin repeated musingly. 'He is a Pole, perhaps?'

His informant laughed a bit shamefacedly. 'Can't say,' he confessed. 'The Serbs weren't asking embarrassing questions about volunteers' nationalities those days, and it wasn't considered healthful for any of us to do so, either. I got the impression he was a Hungarian refugee from Austrian vengeance; but that's only hearsay. Come along, I'll introduce you, if you wish.'

I saw de Grandin clasp hands with the foreigner and stand talking with him for a time, and, in spite of myself, I could not forbear a smile at the contrast they made.

The Frenchman was a bare five feet four inches in height, slender as a girl, and, like a girl, possessed of almost laughably small hands and feet. His light hair and fair skin, coupled with his trimly waxed diminutive blond mustache and round, unwinking blue eyes, gave him a curiously misleading appearance of mildness. His companion was at least six feet tall, swarthy-skinned and black-haired, with bristling black mustaches and fierce, slate-gray eyes set beneath beetling black brows. His large nose was like the predatory beak of some bird of prey, and the tilt of his long, pointed jaw bore out the uncompromising ferocity of the rest of his visage. Across his left cheek, extending upward over the temple and into his hair, was a knife- or saber-scar, a streak of white showing the trail of the steel in his scalp, and shining like silver inlaid in onyx against the blue-black of his smoothly pomaded locks.

What they said was, of course, beyond reach of my ears, but I saw de Grandin's quick, impish smile flicker across his keen face more than once, to be answered by a slow, languorous smile on the other's dark countenance.

At length the count bowed formally to my friend and whirled away with a wisp of a girl, while de Grandin returned to me. At the door he paused a moment, inclining his shoulders in a salute as a couple of debutantes brushed past him. Something – I know not what – drew my attention to the tall foreigner a moment, and a sudden chill rippled up my spine at what I saw. Above the georgette-clad shoulder

SEABURY QUINN

5

of his dancing partner the count's slate-gray eyes were fixed on de Grandin's trim back, and in them I read all the cold, malevolent fury with which a caged tiger regards its keeper as he passes the bars.

'What on earth did you say to that fellow?' I asked as the little Frenchman rejoined me. 'He looked as if he would like to murder you.'

'Ha?' he gave a questioning, single-syllabled laugh. 'Did he so? Obey the noble Washington's injunction, and avoid foreign entanglements, Friend Trowbridge; it is better so, I think.'

'But look here,' I began, nettled by his manner, 'what—'

'*Non, non,*' he interrupted, 'you must be advised by me, my friend. I think it would be better if we dismissed the incident from our minds. But stay – perhaps you had better meet that gentleman, after all. I will have the good Madame Norman introduce you.'

More puzzled than ever, I followed him to our hostess and waited while he requested her to present me to the count.

In a lull in the dancing she complied with his request, and the foreigner acknowledged the introduction with a brief handclasp and an almost churlish nod, then turned his back on me, continuing an animated conversation with the large-eyed young woman in an abbreviated party frock.

'And did you shake his hand?' de Grandin asked as we descended the Normans' steps to my waiting car.

'Yes, of course,' I replied.

'Ah? Tell me, my friend, did you notice anything – ah – peculiar, in his grip?'

'H'm.' I wrinkled my brow a moment in concentrated thought. 'Yes, I believe I did.'

'So? What was it?'

THE MAN WHO CAST NO SHADOW

'Hanged if I can say, exactly,' I admitted, 'but – well, it seemed – this sounds absurd, I know – but it seemed as though his hand had two backs – no palm at all – if that means anything to you.'

'It means much, my friend; it means a very great deal,' he answered with such a solemn nod that I burst into a fit of laughter. 'Believe me, it means much more than you suspect.'

It must have been some two weeks later that I chanced to remark to de Grandin, 'I saw your friend, Count Czerny, in New York yesterday.'

'Indeed?' he answered with what seemed like more than necessary interest. 'And how did he impress you at the time?'

'Oh, I just happened to pass him on Fifth Avenue,' I replied. 'I'd been up to see an acquaintance in Fifty-ninth Street and was turning into the avenue when I saw him driving away from the Plaza. He was with some ladies.'

'No doubt,' de Grandin responded dryly. 'Did you notice him particularly?'

'Can't say that I did, especially,' I answered, 'but it seems to me he looked older than the day we met him at Mrs Norman's.'

'Yes?' the Frenchman leaned forward eagerly. 'Older, do you say? *Parbleu*, this is of interest; I suspected as much!'

'Why—' I began, but he turned away with an impatient shrug.

'Pah!' he exclaimed petulantly. 'Friend Trowbridge, I fear Jules de Grandin is a fool, he entertains all sorts of strange notions.'

I had known the little Frenchman long enough to realize that he was as full of moods as a prima donna, but his erratic,

SEABURY QUINN

7

unrelated remarks were getting on my nerves. 'See here, de Grandin,' I began testily, 'what's all this nonsense—'

The sudden shrill clatter of my office telephone bell cut me short. 'Dr Trowbridge,' an agitated voice asked over the wire, 'can you come right over, please? This is Mrs Norman speaking.'

'Yes, of course,' I answered, reaching for my medicine case; 'what is it – who's ill?'

'It's – it's Guy Eckhart, he's been taken with a fainting fit, and we don't seem to be able to rouse him.'

'Very well,' I promised, 'Dr de Grandin and I will be right over.'

'Come on, de Grandin,' I called as I shoved my hat down over my ears and shrugged into my overcoat, 'one of Mrs Norman's house guests has been taken ill; I told her we were coming.'

'*Mais oui*,' he agreed, hurrying into his outdoors clothes. 'Is it a man or a woman, this sick one?'

'It's a man,' I replied, 'Guy Eckhart.'

'A man,' he echoed incredulously. 'A man, do you say? No, no, my friend, that is not likely.'

'Likely or not,' I rejoined sharply, 'Mrs Norman says he's been seized with a fainting fit, and I give the lady credit for knowing what she's talking about.'

'*Eh bien*,' he drummed nervously on the cushions of the automobile seat, 'perhaps Jules de Grandin really is a fool. After all, it is not impossible.'

'It certainly isn't,' I agreed fervently to myself as I set the car in motion.

Young Eckhart had recovered consciousness when we arrived, but looked like a man just emerging from a lingering fever. Attempts to get a statement from him met with no response, for he replied slowly, almost incoherently, and

THE MAN WHO CAST NO SHADOW

seemed to have no idea concerning the cause of his illness.

Mrs Norman was little more specific. 'My son Ferdinand found him lying on the floor of his bath with the shower going and the window wide open, just before dinner,' she explained. 'He was totally unconscious, and remained so till just a few minutes ago.'

'Ha, is it so?' de Grandin murmured half heedlessly, as he made a rapid inspection of the patient.

'Friend Trowbridge,' he called me to the window, 'what do you make of these objective symptoms: a soft, frequent pulse, a fluttering heart, suffused eyes, a hot, dry skin and a flushed, hectic face?'

'Sounds like an arterial hemorrhage,' I answered promptly, 'but there's been no trace of blood on the boy's floor, nor any evidence of a stain on his clothing. Sure you've checked the signs over?'

'Absolutely,' he replied with a vigorous double nod. Then to the young man: 'Now, *mon enfant*, we shall inspect you, if you please.'

Quickly he examined the boy's face, scalp, throat, wrists and calves, finding no evidence of even a pinprick, let alone a wound capable of causing syncope.

'*Mon Dieu*, this is strange,' he muttered; 'of a surety, it has the queerness of the devil! Perhaps the bleeding is internal, but – ah, *regardez vous*, Friend Trowbridge!'

He had turned down the collar of the youngster's pajama jacket, more in idle routine than in hope of discovering anything tangible, but the livid spot to which he pointed seemed the key to our mystery's outer door. Against the smooth, white flesh of the young man's left breast there showed a red, angry patch, such as might have resulted from a vacuum cup being held some time against the skin, and in

SEABURY QUINN

9

the center of the discoloration was a double row of tiny punctures scarcely larger than needle-pricks, arranged in horizontal divergent arcs, like a pair of parentheses laid sidewise.

'You see?' he asked simply, as though the queer, blood-infused spot explained everything.

'But he couldn't have bled much through that,' I protested. 'Why, the man seems almost drained dry, and these wounds wouldn't have yielded more than a cubic centimeter of blood, at most.'

He nodded gravely. 'Blood is not entirely colloidal, my friend,' he responded. 'It will penetrate the tissues to some extent, especially if sufficient force is applied.'

'But it would have required a powerful suction—' I replied, when his rejoinder cut me short:

'Ha, you have said it, my friend. Suction – that is the word!'

'But what could have sucked a man's blood like this?' I was in a near-stupor of mystification.

'What, indeed?' he replied gravely. 'That is for us to find out. Meantime, we are here as physicians. A quarter-grain morphine injection is indicated here, I think. You will administer the dose; I have no license in America.'

When I returned from my round of afternoon calls next day I found de Grandin seated on my front steps in close conference with Indian John.

Indian John was a town character of doubtful lineage who performed odd jobs of snow shoveling, furnace tending and grass cutting, according to season, and interspersed his manual labors with brief incursions into the mercantile field when he peddled fresh vegetables from door to door. He also peddled neighborhood gossip and retailed local lore

THE MAN WHO CAST NO SHADOW

to all who would listen, his claim to being a hundred years old giving him the standing of an indisputable authority in all matters antedating living memory.

'*Pardieu*, but you have told me much, *mon vieux*,' de Grandin declared as I came up the porch steps. He handed the old rascal a handful of silver and rose to accompany me into the house.

'Friend Trowbridge,' he accused as we finished dinner that night, 'you had not told me that this town grew up on the site of an early Swedish settlement.'

'Never knew you wanted to know,' I defended with a grin.

'You know the ancient Swedish church, perhaps,' he persisted.

'Yes, that's old Christ Church,' I answered. 'It's down in the east end of town; don't suppose it has a hundred communicants today. Our population has made some big changes, both in complexion and creed, since the days when the Dutch and Swedes fought for possession of New Jersey.'

'You will drive me to that church, right away, at once, immediately?' he demanded eagerly.

'I guess so,' I agreed. 'What's the matter now; Indian John been telling you a lot of fairy-tales?'

'Perhaps,' he replied, regarding me with one of his steady, unwinking stares. 'Not all fairy-tales are pleasant, you know. Do you recall those of *Chaperon Rouge* – how do you say it, Red Riding Hood? – and Bluebeard?'

'Huh!' I scoffed; 'they're both as true as any of John's stories, I'll bet.'

'Undoubtlessly,' he agreed with a quick nod. 'The story of Bluebeard, for instance, is unfortunately a very true tale indeed. But come, let us hasten; I would see that church tonight, if I may.'

SEABURY QUINN

11

Christ Church, the old Swedish place of worship, was a combined demonstration of how firmly adzhewn pine and walnut can resist the ravages of time and how nearly three hundred years of weather can demolish any structure erected by man. Its rough-painted walls and short, firm-based spire shone ghostly and pallid in the early spring moonlight, and the cluster of broken and weather-worn tombstones which staggered up from its unkempt burying ground were like soiled white chicks seeking shelter from a soiled white hen.

Dismounting from a car at the wicket gate of the churchyard, we made our way over the level graves, I in a maze of wonderment, de Grandin with an eagerness almost childish. Occasionally he flashed the beam from his electric torch on some monument of an early settler, bent to decipher the worn inscription, then turned away with a sigh of disappointment.

I paused to light a cigar, but dropped my half-burned match in astonishment as my companion gave vent to a cry of excited pleasure. '*Triomphe!*' he exclaimed delightedly. 'Come and behold, Friend Trowbridge. Thus far your lying friend, the Indian man, has told the truth. *Regardez!*'

He was standing beside an old, weather-gnawed tombstone, once marble, perhaps, but appearing more like brown sandstone under the ray of his flashlight. Across its upper end was deeply cut the one word:

SARAH

while below the name appeared a verse of half-obliterated doggerel:

THE MAN WHO CAST NO SHADOW

12

Let nonne difturb her deathleffe fleepe
Abote ye tombe wilde garlick keepe
For if fhee wake much woe will boaft
Prayfe Faither, Sonne & Holie Goaft.

'Did you bring me out here to study the orthographical eccentricities of the early settlers?' I demanded in disgust.

'Ah bah!' he returned. 'Let us consult the *ecclésiastique*. He, perhaps, will ask no fool's questions.'

'No, you'll do that,' I answered tartly as we knocked at the rectory door.

'Pardon, *Monsieur*,' de Grandin apologized as the white-haired old minister appeared in answer to our summons, 'we do not wish to disturb you thus, but there is a matter of great import on which we would consult you. I would that you tell us what you can, if anything, concerning a certain grave in your churchyard. A grave marked "Sarah", if you please.'

'Why' – the elderly cleric was plainly taken aback – 'I don't think there is anything I can tell you about it, sir. There is some mention in the early parish records, I believe, of a woman believed to have been a murderess being buried in that grave, but it seems the poor creature was more sinned against than sinning. Several children in the neighborhood died mysteriously – some epidemic the ignorant physicians failed to understand, no doubt – and Sarah, whatever the poor woman's surname may have been, was accused of killing them by witchcraft. At any rate, one of the bereft mothers took vengeance into her own hands, and strangled poor Sarah with a noose of well-rope. The witchcraft belief must have been quite prevalent, too, for there is some nonsense verse on the tombstone concerning her "deathless sleep" and an allusion to her waking from it;

SEABURY QUINN

13

also some mention of wild garlic being planted about her.'

He laughed somewhat ruefully. 'I wish they hadn't said that,' he added, 'for, do you know, there are garlic shoots growing about that grave to this very day. Old Christian, our sexton, declares that he can't get rid of it, no matter how much he grubs it up. It spreads to the surrounding lawn, too,' he added sadly.

'*Cordieu!*' de Grandin gasped. 'This is of the importance, sir!'

The old man smiled gently at the little Frenchman's impetuosity.

'It's an odd thing,' he commented, 'there was another gentleman asking about that same tomb a few weeks ago; a – pardon the expression – a foreigner.'

'So?' de Grandin's little, waxed mustache twitched like the whiskers of a nervous tom-cat. 'A foreigner, do you say? A tall, rawboned, fleshless living skeleton of a man with a scar on his face and a white streak in his hair?'

'I wouldn't be quite so severe in my description,' the other answered with a smile. 'He certainly was a thin gentleman, and I believe he had a scar on his face, too, though I can't be certain of that, he was so very wrinkled. No, his hair was entirely white, there was no white streak in ·it, sir. In fact, I should have said he was very advanced in age, judging from his hair and face and the manner in which he walked. He seemed very weak and feeble. It was really quite pitiable.'

'*Sacre nom d'un fromage vert!*' de Grandin almost snarled. 'Pitiable, do you say, *Monsieur? Pardieu*, it is damnable, nothing less!'

He bowed to the clergyman and turned to me. 'Come, Friend Trowbridge, come away,' he cried. 'We must go to Madame Norman's at once, right away, immediately.'

THE MAN WHO CAST NO SHADOW

'What's behind all this mystery?' I demanded as we left the parsonage door.

He elevated his slender shoulders in an eloquent shrug. 'I only wish I knew,' he replied. 'Someone is working the devil's business, of that I am sure; but what the game is, or what the next move will be, only the good God can tell, my friend.'

I turned the car through Tunlaw Street to effect a short-cut, and as we drove past an Italian greengrocer's, de Grandin seized my arm. 'Stop a moment, Friend Trow-bridge,' he asked, 'I would make a purchase at this shop.'

'We desire some fresh garlic,' he informed the proprietor as we entered the little store, 'a considerable amount, if you have it.'

The Italian spread his hands in a deprecating gesture. 'We have it not, *Signor*,' he declared. 'It was only yesterday morning that we sold our entire supply.' His little black eyes snapped happily at the memory of an unexpected bargain.

'Eh, what is this?' de Grandin demanded. 'Do you say you sold your supply? How is that?'

'I know not,' the other replied. 'Yesterday morning a rich gentleman came to my shop in an automobile, and called me from my store. He desired all the garlic I had in stock – at my own price, *Signor*, and at once. I was to deliver it to his address in Rupleysville the same day.'

'Ah?' de Grandin's face assumed the expression of a cross-word fiend as he begins to see the solution of his puzzle. 'And this liberal purchaser, what did he look like?'

The Italian showed his white, even teeth in a wide grin. 'It was funny,' he confessed. 'He did not look like one of our people, nor like one who would eat much garlic. He was old, very old and thin, with a much-wrinkled face and white hair, he—'

15

'*Nom d'un chat!*' the Frenchman cried, then burst into a flood of torrential Italian.

The shopkeeper listened at first with suspicion, then incredulity, finally in abject terror. 'No, no,' he exclaimed. 'No, *Signor*; *santissima Madonna*, you do make the joke!'

'Do I so?' de Grandin replied. 'Wait and see, foolish one.'

'*Santo Dio* forbid!' The other crossed himself piously, then bent his thumb across his palm, circling it with his second and third fingers and extending the fore and little fingers in the form of a pair of horns.

The Frenchman turned toward the waiting car with a grunt of inarticulate disgust.

'What now?' I asked as we got under way once more; 'what did that man make the sign of the evil eye for, de Grandin?'

'Later, my friend; I will tell you later,' he answered. 'You would but laugh if I told you what I suspect. He is of the Latin blood, and can appreciate my fears.' Nor would he utter another word till we reached the Norman house.

'Dr Trowbridge – Dr de Grandin!' Mrs Norman met us in the hall; 'you must have heard my prayers; I've been phoning your office for the last hour, and they said you were out and couldn't be reached.'

'What's up?' I asked.

'It's Mr Eckhart again. He's been seized with another fainting fit. He seemed so well this afternoon, and I sent a big dinner up to him at 8 o'clock, but when the maid went in, she found him unconscious, and she declares she saw something in his room—'

'Ha?' de Grandin interrupted. 'Where is she, this servant? I would speak with her.'

'Wait a moment,' Mrs Norman answered; 'I'll send for her.'

The girl, an ungainly young Southern negress, came into

THE MAN WHO CAST NO SHADOW

the front hall, sullen dissatisfaction written large upon her black face.

'Now, then,' de Grandin bent his steady, unwinking gaze on her, 'what is it you say about seeing someone in the young Monsieur Eckhart's room, *hein?*'

'Ah did see sumpin', too,' the girl replied stubbornly. 'Ah don' care who says Ah didn't see nothin', Ah says Ah did. Ah'd just toted a tray o' vittles up to Mistuh Eckhart's room, an' when Ah opened de do', dere wuz a woman – dere wuz a woman – yas, sar, a skinny, black-eyed white woman – a-bendin' ober 'um an' – an'—'

'And what, if you please?' de Grandin asked breathlessly.

'A-bitin' 'um!' the girl replied defiantly. 'Ah don' car whut Mis' Norman says, she wuz a-bitin' 'um. Ah seen her. Ah knows whut she wuz. Ah done hyeah tell erbout dat ol' Sarah woman what come up out 'er grave wid a long rope erbout her neck and go 'round bitin' folks. Yas, sar; an' she wuz a-bitin' 'um, too. Ah seen her!'

'Nonsense,' Mrs Norman commented in an annoyed whisper over de Grandin's shoulder.

'*Grand Dieu*, is it so?' de Grandin explained, and turning abruptly, leaped up the stairs toward the sick man's room, two steps at a time.

'See, see, Friend Trowbridge,' he ordered fiercely when I joined him at the patient's bedside. 'Behold, it is the mark!' Turning back Eckhart's pajama collar, he displayed two incised horizontal arcs on the young man's flesh. There was no room for dispute, they were undoubtedly the marks of human teeth, and from the fresh wounds the blood was flowing freely.

As quickly as possible we staunched the flow and applied restoratives to the patient, both of us working in silence, for my brain was too much in a whirl to permit the formation

SEABURY QUINN

17

of intelligent questions, while de Grandin remained dumb as an oyster.

'Now,' he ordered as we completed our ministrations, 'we must get back to that cemetery, Friend Trowbridge, and once there, we must do the thing which must be done!'

'What the devil's that?' I asked as we left the sickroom.

'*Non, non*, you shall see,' he promised as we entered my car and drove down the street.

'Quick, the crank-handle,' he demanded as we descended from the car at the cemetery gate, 'it will make a serviceable hammer.' He was prying a hemlock paling from the graveyard fence as he spoke.

We crossed the unkempt cemetery lawn again and finally paused beside the tombstone of the unknown Sarah.

'Attend me, Friend Trowbridge,' de Grandin commanded, 'hold the searchlight, if you please.' He pressed his pocket flash into my hand. 'Now—' He knelt beside the grave, pointing the stick he had wrenched from the fence straight downward into the turf. With the crank of my motor he began hammering the wood into the earth.

Farther and farther the rough stake sank into the sod, de Grandin's blows falling faster and faster as the wood drove home. Finally, when there was less than six inches of the wicket projecting from the grave's top, he raised the iron high over his head and drove downward with all his might.

The short hair at the back of my neck suddenly started upward, and little thrills of horripilation chased each other up my spine as the wood sank suddenly, as though driven from clay into sand, and a low hopeless moan, like the wailing of a frozen wind through an ice-cave, wafted up to us from the depths of the grave.

'Good God, what's that?' I asked, aghast.

For answer he leaned forward, seized the stake in both

THE MAN WHO CAST NO SHADOW

hands and drew suddenly up on it. At his second tug the wood came away. 'See,' he ordered curtly, flashing the pocket lamp on the tip of the stave. For the distance of a foot or so from its pointed end the wood was stained a deep, dull red. It was wet with blood.

'And now forever,' he hissed between his teeth, driving the wood into the grave once more, and sinking it a full foot below the surface of the grass by thrusting the crank-handle into the earth. 'Come, Friend Trowbridge, we have done a good work this night. I doubt not the young Eckhart will soon recover from his malady.'

His assumption was justified. Eckhart's condition improved steadily. Within a week, save for a slight pallor, he was, to all appearances, as well as ever.

The pressure of the usual early crop of influenza and pneumonia kept me busily on my rounds, and I gradually gave up hope of getting any information from de Grandin, for a shrug of the shoulders was all the answer he vouchsafed to my questions. I relegated Eckhart's inexplicable hemorrhages and the bloodstained stake to the limbo of never-to-be-solved mysteries. But—

2

'Good mornin', gentlemen,' Detective Sergeant Costello greeted as he followed Nora, my household factorum, into the breakfast room, 'it's sorry I am to be disturbin' your meal, but there's a little case puzzlin' th' department that I'd like to talk over with Dr de Grandin, if you don't mind.'

He looked expectantly at the little Frenchman as he finished speaking, his lips parted to launch upon a detailed description of the case.

SEABURY QUINN

'*Parbleu*,' de Grandin laughed, 'it is fortunate for me that I have completed my breakfast, *cher Sergent*, for a riddle of crime detection is to me like a red rag to a bullfrog – I must needs snap at it, whether I have been fed or no. Speak on, my friend, I beseech you; I am like Balaam's ass, all ears.'

The big Irishman seated himself on the extreme edge of one of my Heppelwhite chairs and gazed deprecatingly at the derby he held firmly between his knees. 'It's like this,' he began, ''tis one o' them mysterious disappearance cases, gentleman an' whilst I'm thinkin' th' young lady knows exactly where she's at an' why she's there, I hate to tell her folks about it.

'All th' high-hat folks ain't like you two gentlemen, askin' your pardon, sors – they mostly seems to think that a harness bull's unyform is sumpin' like a livery – like a shofur's or a footman's or sumpin', an' that a plainclothes man is just a sort o' inferior servant. They don't give th' police credit for no brains, y'see, an' when one o' their darters gits giddy an' runs off th' reservation, if we tells 'em th' gurrl's run away of her own free will an' accord they say we're a lot o' lazy, good-fer-nothin' bums who are tryin' to dodge our laygitimate jooties by castin' mud on th' young ladies' char-acters, d'ye see? So, when this Miss Esther Norman disappears in broad daylight – leastwise, in th' twilight – o' th' day before her dance, we suspects right away that th' gurrl's gone her own ways into th' best o' intentions, y'see; but we dasn't tell her folks as much, or they'll be hollerin' to th' commissioner fer to git a bran' new set o' detectives down to headquarters, so they will.

'Now, mind ye, I'm not sayin' th' young lady *mightn't* o' been kidnapped, y'understand, gentlemen, but I do be sayin' 'tis most unlikely. I've been on th' force, man an' boy, in unyform and in plain clothes fer th' last twenty-five years, an'

THE MAN WHO CAST NO SHADOW

th' number of laygitimate kidnapin's o' young women over ten years of age I've seen can be counted on th' little finger o' me left hand, an' I ain't got none there, at all, at all.'

He held the member up for our inspection, revealing the fact that the little finger had been amputated close to the knuckle.

De Grandin, elbows on the table, pointed chin cupped in his hands, was puffing furiously at a vile-smelling French cigarette, alternately sucking down great drafts of its acrid smoke and expelling clouds of fumes in double jets from his narrow, aristocratic nostrils.

'What is it you say?' he demanded, removing the cigarette from his lips. 'Is it the so lovely *Mademoiselle* Esther, daughter of that kind Madame Tuscarora Avenue Norman, who is missing?'

'Yes, sor,' Costello answered, ''tis th' same young lady's flew the coop, accordin' to my way o' thinkin'.'

'*Mordieu!*' the Frenchman gave the ends of his blond mustache a savage twist; 'you intrigue me, my friend. Say on, how did it happen, and when?'

''Twas about midnight last night th' alarm came into headquarters,' the detective replied. 'Accordin' to th' facts as we have 'em, th' young lady went downtown in th' Norman car to do some errands. We've checked her movements up, an' here they are.'

He drew a black-leather memorandum book from his pocket and consulted it.

'At 2:45 or thereabouts, she left th' house, arrivin' at th' Ocean Trust Company at 2:55, five minutes before th' instytootion closed for th' day. She drew out three hundred an' thirty dollars an' sixty-five cents, an' left th' bank, goin' to Madame Gerard's, where she tried on a party dress for th' dance which was bein' given at her house that night.

'She left Madame Gerard's at 4:02, leavin' orders for th' dress to be delivered to her house immeejately, an' dismissed her sho-fur at th' corner o' Dean an' Tunlaw Streets, sayin' she was goin' to deliver some vegytables an' what-not to a pore family she an' some o' her friends was keepin' till their oldman gits let out o' jail – twas meself an' Clancey, me buddy, that put him there when we caught him red-handed in a job o' housebreakin', too.

'Well, to return to th' young lady, she stopped at Pete Bacigalupo's store in Tunlaw Street an' bought a basket o' fruit an' canned things, at 4:30, an'—' He clamped his long-suffering derby between his knees and spread his hands emptily before us.

'Yes, "and"—?' de Grandin prompted, dropping the glowing end of his cigarette into his coffee cup.

'An' that's all,' responded the Irishman. 'She just walked off, an' no one ain't seen her since, sor.'

'But – *cordieu!* – such things do not occur, my friend,' de Grandin protested. 'Somewhere you have overlooked a factor in this puzzle. You say no one saw her later? Have you nothing whatever to add to the tale?'

'Well' – the detective grinned at him – 'there are one or two little incidents, but they ain't of any importance in th' case, as far as I can see. Just as she left Pete's store an old gink tried to "make" her, but she give him th' air, an' he went off an' didn't bother her no more.

'I'd a' liked to seen th' old boy, at that. Day before yesterday there was an old felly hangin' 'round by the silk mills, annoyin' th' gurrls as they come off from work. Clancey, me mate, saw 'im an' started to take 'im up, an' darned if th' old rummy wasn't strong as a bull. D'ye know, he broke clean away from Clancey an' darn near broke his

THE MAN WHO CAST NO SHADOW

arm, in th' bargain? Belike 'twas th' same man accosted Miss Norman outside Pete's store.'

'Ah?' de Grandin's slender, white fingers began beating a devil's tattoo on the tablecloth. 'And who was it saw this old man annoy the lady *hein?*'

Costello grinned widely, ''Twas Peter Bacigalupo himself, sor,' he answered. 'Pete swore he recognized th' old geezer as havin' come to his store a month or so ago in an autymobile an bought up all his entire stock o' garlic. Huh! Th' fool dago said he wouldn't a gone after th' felly for a hundred dollars – said he had th' pink-eye, or th' evil eye, or some such thing. Them wops sure do burn me up!'

'*Dieu et le diable!*' de Grandin leaped up, oversetting his chair in his mad haste. 'And we sit here like three *poissons d'avril* – like poor fish – while he works his devilish will on her! Quick, Sergeant! Quick, Friend Trowbridge! Your hats, your coats; the motor! Oh, make haste, my friends, fly, fly, I implore you; even now it may be too late!'

As though all the fiends of pandemonium were at his heels he raced from the breakfast room, up the stairs, three steps at a stride, and down the upper hall toward his bedroom. Nor did he cease his shouted demands for haste throughout his wild flight.

'Cuckoo?' The sergeant tapped his forehead significantly.

I shook my head as I hastened to the hall for my driving clothes. 'No,' I answered, shrugging into my topcoat, 'he's got a reason for everything he does; but you and I can't always see it, Sergeant.'

'You said a mouthful that time, doc,' he agreed, pulling his hat down over his ears. 'He's the darndest, craziest Frog I ever seen, but, at that, he's got more sense than nine men out o'ten.'

'To Rupleysville, Friend Trowbridge,' de Grandin shouted

as he leaped into the seat beside me. 'Make haste, I do implore you. Oh, Jules de Grandin, your grandfäther was an imbecile and all your ancestors were idiots, but you are the greatest zany in the family. Why, oh, why, do you require a sunstroke before you can see the light, foolish one?'

I swung the machine down the pike at highest legal speed, but the little Frenchman kept urging greater haste. '*Sang de Dieu, sang de Saint Denis, sang du diable!*' he wailed despairingly. 'Can you not make this abominable car go faster, Friend Trowbridge? Oh, ah, *helas*, if we are too late! I shall hate myself, I shall loathe myself – *pardieu*, I shall become a Carmelite friar and eat fish and abstain from swearing!'

We took scarcely twenty minutes to cover the ten-mile stretch to the aggregation of tumbledown houses which was Rupleysville, but my companion was almost frothing at the mouth when I drew up before the local apology for a hotel.

'Tell me, *Monsieur*,' de Grandin cried as he thrust the hostelry's door open with his foot and brandished his slender ebony cane before the astonished proprietor's eyes, 'tell me of *un vieillard* – an old, old man with snow-white hair and an evil face, who has lately come to this so detestable place. I would know where to find him, right away, immediately, at once!'

'Say,' the boniface demanded truculently, 'where d'ye git that stuff? Who are you to be askin'—'

'That'll do' – Costello shouldered his way past de Grandin and displayed his badge – 'you answer this gentleman's questions, an' answer 'em quick an' accurate, or I'll run you in, see?'

The innkeeper's defiant attitude melted before the

THE MAN WHO CAST NO SHADOW

detective's show of authority like frost before the sunrise. 'Guess you must mean Mr Zerny,' he replied sullenly. 'He come here about a month ago an' rented the Hazeltown house, down th' road about a mile. Comes up to town for provisions every day or two, and stops in here sometimes for a—' He halted abruptly, his face suffused with a dull flush.

'Yeah?' Costello replied. 'Go on an' say it; we all know what he stops here for. Now listen, buddy' – he stabbed the air two inches before the man's face with a blunt forefinger – 'I don't know whether this here Zerny felly's got a tellyphone or not, but if he has, you just lay off tellin' 'im we're comin'; git me? If anyone's tipped him off when we git to his place I'm comin' back here and plaster more padlocks on this place o' yours than Sousa's got medals on his blouse. Savvy?'

'Come away, *Sergent*; come away, Friend Trowbridge,' de Grandin besought almost tearfully. 'Bandy not words with the *cancre*; we have work to do!'

Down the road we raced in the direction indicated by the hotelkeeper, till the picket fence and broken shutters of the Hazelton house showed among a rank copse of second-growth pines at the bend of the highway.

The shrewd wind of early spring was moaning and soughing among the black boughs of the pine trees as we ran toward the house, and though it was bright with sunshine on the road, there was chill and shadow about us as we climbed the sagging steps of the old building's ruined piazza and paused breathlessly before the paintless front door.

'Shall I knock?' Costello asked dubiously, involuntarily sinking his voice to a whisper.

'But no,' de Grandin answered in a low voice, 'what we have to do here must be done quietly, my friends.'

He leaned forward and tried the doorknob with a light,

SEABURY QUINN

25

tentative touch. The door gave under his hand, swinging inward on protesting hinges, and we tiptoed into a dark, dust-carpeted hall. A shaft of sunlight, slanting downward from a chink in one of the window shutters, showed innumerable dust-motes flying lazily in the air, and laid a bright oval of light against the warped floor-boards.

'Huh, empty as a pork-butcher's in Jerusalem,' Costello commented disgustedly, looking about the unfurnished rooms, but de Grandin seized him by the elbow with one hand while he pointed toward the floor with the ferrule of his slender ebony walking stick.

'Empty, perhaps,' he conceded in a low, vibrant whisper, 'but not recently, *mon ami*.' Where the sunbeam splashed on the uneven floor there showed distinctly the mark of a booted foot, two marks – a trail of them leading toward the rear of the house.

'Right y'are,' the detective agreed. 'Someone's left his track here, an' no mistake.'

'Ha!' de Grandin bent forward till it seemed the tip of his highbridged nose would impinge on the tracks. 'Gentlemen,' he rose and pointed forward into the gloom with a dramatic flourish of his cane, 'they are here! Let us go!'

Through the gloomy hall we followed the trail by the aid of Costello's flashlight, stepping carefully to avoid creaking boards as much as possible. At length the marks stopped abruptly in the center of what had formerly been the kitchen. A disturbance in the dust told where the walker had doubled on his tracks in a short circle, and a ringbolt in the floor gave notice that we stood above a trap-door of some sort.

'Careful, Friend Costello,' de Grandin warned, 'have ready your flashlight when I fling back the trap. Ready? *Un – deux – trois!*'

He bent, seized the rusty ringbolt and heaved the trap-door back so violently that it flew back with a thundering crash on the floor beyond.

The cavern had originally been a cellar for the storage of food, it seemed, and was brick-walled and earth-floored, without window or ventilation opening of any sort. A dank, musty odor assaulted our nostrils as we leaned forward, but further impressions were blotted out by the sight directly beneath us.

White as a figurine of carven alabaster, the slender, bare body of a girl lay in sharp reverse silhouette against the darkness of the cavern floor, her ankles crossed and firmly lashed to a stake in the earth, one hand doubled behind her back in the position of a wrestler's hammerlock grip, and made firm to a peg in the floor, while the left arm was extended straight outward, its wrist pinioned to another stake. Her luxuriant fair hair had been knotted together at the ends, then staked to the ground, so that her head was drawn far back, exposing her rounded throat to its fullest extent, and on the earth beneath her left breast and beside her throat stood two porcelain bowls.

Crouched over her was the relic of a man, an old, old, hideously wrinkled witch-husband, with matted white hair and beard. In one hand he held a long, gleaming, double-edged dirk while with the other he caressed the girl's smooth throat with gloating strokes of his skeleton fingers.

'Howly Mither!' Costello's County Galway brogue broke through his American accent at the horrid sight below us.

'My God!' I exclaimed, all the breath in my lungs suddenly seeming to freeze in my throat.

'*Bonjour, Monsieur le Vampire!*' Jules de Grandin greeted nonchalantly, leaping to the earth beside the pinioned girl and waving his walking stick airily. 'By the horns of the devil, but you have led us a merry chase, Baron

SEABURY QUINN

27

Lajos Czuczron of Transylvania!'

The crouching creature emitted a bellow of fury and leaped toward de Grandin, brandishing his knife.

The Frenchman gave ground with a quick, catlike leap and grasped his slender cane in both hands near the top. Next instant he had ripped the lower part of the stick away, displaying a fine, three-edged blade set in the cane's handle, and swung his point toward the frothing-mouthed thing which mouthed and gibbered like a beast at bay. 'A-ah?' he cried with a mocking, upward-lilting accent. 'You did not expect this, eh, Friend Blood-drinker? I give you the party-of-surprize, *n'est-ce-pas?* The centuries have been long, *mon vieux;* but the reckoning has come at last. Say, now will you die by the steel, or by starvation?'

The aged monster fairly champed his gleaming teeth in fury. His eyes seemed larger, rounder, to gleam like the eyes of a dog in the firelight, as he launched himself toward the little Frenchman.

'*Sa-ha!*' the Frenchman sank backward on one foot, then straightened suddenly forward, stiffening his sword-arm and plunging his point directly into the charging beastman's distended, red mouth. A scream of mingled rage and pain filled the cavern with deafening shrillness, and the monster half turned, as though on an invisible pivot, clawed with horrid impotence at the wire-fine blade of de Grandin's rapier, then sank slowly to the earth, his death cry stilled to a sickening gurgle as his throat filled with blood.

'*Fini!*' de Grandin commented laconically, drawing out his handkerchief and wiping his blade with meticulous care, then cutting the unconscious girl's bonds with his pocket-knife. 'Drop down your overcoat, Friend Trowbridge,' he added, 'that we may cover the poor child's nudity until we can piece out a wardrobe for her.'

THE MAN WHO CAST NO SHADOW

'Now, then' – as he raised her to meet the hands Costello and I extended into the pit – 'if we clothe her in the motor rug, your jacket, *Sergent*, Friend Trowbridge's topcoat and my shoes, she will be safe from the chill. *Parbleu*, I have seen women refugees from the Boche who could not boast so complete a toilette!'

With Esther Norman, hastily clothed in her patchwork assortment of garments, wedged in the front seat between de Grandin and me, we began our triumphant journey home.

'An' would ye mind tellin' me how ye knew where to look for th' young lady, Dr de Grandin, sor?' Detective Sergeant Costello asked respectfully, leaning forward from the rear seat of the car.

'Wait, wait, my friend,' de Grandin replied with a smile. 'When our duties are all performed I shall tell you such a tale as shall make your two eyes to pop outward like a snail's. First, however, you must go with us to restore this *pauvre enfant* to her mother's arms; then to the headquarters to report the death of that *sale bête*. Friend Trowbridge will stay with the young lady for so long as he deems necessary, and I shall remain with him to help. Then, this evening – with your consent, Friend Trowbridge – you will dine with us, *Sergent*, and I shall tell you all, everything, in total. Death of my life, what a tale it is! *Parbleu*, but you shall call me a liar many times before it is finished!'

Jules de Grandin placed his demitasse on the tabouret and refilled his liqueur glass. 'My friends,' he began, turning his quick, elfish smile first on Costello, then on me, 'I have promised you a remarkable tale. Very well, then, to begin.'

He flicked a wholly imaginary fleck of dust from his dinner jacket sleeve and crossed his slender, womanishly small feet on the hearth rug.

SEABURY QUINN

29

'Do you recall, Friend Trowbridge, how we went, you and I, to the tea given by the good Madame Norman? Yes? Perhaps, then, you will recall how at the entrance of the ballroom I stopped with a look of astonishment on my face. Very good. At that moment I saw that which made me disbelieve the evidence of my own two eyes. As the gentleman we later met as Count Czerny danced past a mirror on the wall I beheld – *parbleu!* what do you suppose? – the reflection only of his dancing partner! It was as if the man had been non-existent, and the young lady had danced past the mirror by herself.

'Now, such a thing was not likely, I admit; you, *Sergent*, and you, too, Friend Trowbridge, will say it was not possible; but such is not the case. In certain circumstances it is possible for that which we see with our eyes to cast no shadow in a mirror. Let that point wait a moment; we have other evidence to consider first.

'When the young man told us of the count's prowess in battle, of his incomparable ferocity, I began to believe that which I had at first disbelieved, and when he told us the count was a Hungarian, I began to believe more than ever.

'I met the count, as you will remember, and I took his hand in mine. *Parbleu*, it was like a hand with no palm – it had hairs on both sides of it! You, too, Friend Trowbridge, remarked on that phenomenon.

'While I talked with him I managed to manoeuver him before a mirror. *Morbleu*, the man was as if he had not been; I could see my own face smiling at me where I knew I should have seen the reflection of his shoulder!

'Now, attend me: The *Sûreté Générale* – what you call the Police Headquarters – of Paris is not like your English and American bureaus. All facts, no matter however seemingly absurd, which come to that office are carefully noted down for future reference. Among other histories I have read in the archives of that office was that of one Baron Lajos Czuczron of Transylvania, whose actions had once been watched by our secret agents.

'This man was rich and favored beyond the common run of Hungarian petty nobles, but he was far from beloved by his peasantry. He was known as cruel, wicked and implacable, and no one could be found who had ever one kind word to say for him.

'Half the countryside suspected him of being a *loup-garou*, or werewolf, the others credited a local legend that a woman of his family had once in the olden days taken a demon to husband and that he was the offspring of that unholy union. According to the story, the progeny of this wicked woman lived like an ordinary man for one hundred years, then died on the stroke of the century *unless his vitality was renewed by drinking the blood of a slaughtered virgin!*

'Absurd? Possibly. An English intelligence office would have said "bally nonsense" if one of its agents had sent in such a report. An American bureau would have labeled the report as being the sauce-of-the-apple; but consider this fact: in six hundred years there was no single record of a Baron Czuczron having died. Barons grew old – old to the point of death – but always there came along a new baron, a man in the prime of life, not a youth, to take the old baron's place, nor could any say when the old baron had died or where his body had been laid.

'Now, I had been told that a man under a curse – the werewolf, the vampire, or any other thing in man's shape who lives more than his allotted time by virtue of wickedness – can not cast a shadow in a mirror; also that those accursed ones have hair in the palms of their hands. *Eh bien*,

SEABURY QUINN

31

with this foreknowledge, I engaged this man who called himself Count Czerny in conversation concerning Transylvania. *Parbleu*, the fellow denied all knowledge of the country. He denied it with more force than was necessary. "You are a liar, *Monsieur le Comte*," I tell him, but I say it to myself. Even yet, however, I do not think what I think later.

'Then came the case of the young Eckhart. He loses blood, he can not say how or why, but Friend Trowbridge and I find a queer mark on his body. I think to me, "if, perhaps, a vampire – a member of that accursed tribe who leave their graves by night and suck the blood of the living – were here, that would account for this young man's condition. But where would such a being come from? It is not likely."

'Then I meet that old man, the one you call Indian John. He tells me much of the history of this town in the early days, and he tells me something more. He tells of a man, an old, old man, who has paid him much money to go to a certain grave – the grave of a reputed witch – in the old cemetery and dig from about it a growth of wild garlic. Garlic, I know is a plant intolerable to the vampire. He can not abide it. If it is planted on his grave he can not pass it.

'I ask myself, "Who would want such a thing to be, and why?" But I have no answer; only, I know, if a vampire have been confined to that grave by planted garlic, then liberated when that garlic is taken away, it would account for the young Eckhart's strange sickness.

'*Tiens*, Friend Trowbridge and I visit that grave, and on its tombstone we read a verse which makes me believe the tenant of that grave may be a vampire. We interview the good minister of the church and learn that another man, an old, old man, have also inquired about that strange grave.

THE MAN WHO CAST NO SHADOW

"Who have done this?" I ask me; but even yet I have no definite answer to my question.

'As we rush to the Norman house to see young Eckhart I stop at an Italian green grocer's and ask for fresh garlic, for I think perhaps we can use it to protect the young Eckhart if it really is a vampire which is troubling him. *Parbleu,* some man, an old, old man, have what you Americans call "cornered" the available supply of garlic. "*Cordieu,*" I tell me, "this old man, he constantly crosses our trail! Also he is a very great nuisance."

'The Italian tell me the garlic was sent to a house in Rupleysville, so I have an idea where this interfering old rascal may abide. But at that moment I have greater need to see our friend Eckhart than to ask further questions of the Italian. Before I go, however, I tell that shopkeeper that his garlic customer has the evil eye. *Parbleu, Monsieur* Garlic-Buyer you will have no more dealings with that Italian! He knows what he knows.

'When we arrive at the Norman house we find young Eckhart in great trouble, and a black serving maid tells of a strange-looking woman who bit him. Also, we find tooth-marks on his breast. "The vampire woman, Sarah, is, in the very truth, at large," I tell me, and so I hasten to the cemetery to make her fast to her grave with a wooden stake, for, once he is staked down, the vampire can no longer roam. He is finished.

'Friend Trowbridge will testify he saw blood on the stake driven into a grave dug nearly three hundred years ago. Is it not so, *mon ami?*'

I nodded assent, and he took up his narrative:

'Why this old man should wish to liberate the vampire-woman, I know not; certain it is, one of that grisly guild, or one closely associated with it, as this "Count Czerny"

SEABURY QUINN

undoubtedly was, can tell when another of the company is in the vicinity, and I doubt not he did this deed for pure malice and deviltry.

'However that may be, Friend Trowbridge tells me he have seen the count, and that he seems to have aged greatly. The man who visited the clergyman and the man who bought the garlic was also much older than the count as we knew him. "Ah ha, he is coming to the end of his century," I tell me; "now look out for devilment, Jules de Grandin. Certainly, it is sure to come."

'And then, my *Sergent*, come you with your tale of *Mademoiselle* Norman's disappearance, and I, too, think perhaps she has run away from home voluntarily, of her own free will, until you say the Italian shopkeeper recognized the old man who accosted her as one who has the evil eye. Now what old man, save the one who bought the garlic and who lives at Rupleysville, would that Italian accuse of the evil eye? *Pardieu*, has he not already told you the same man once bought his garlic? But yes. The case is complete.

'The girl has disappeared, an old, old man has accosted her; an old, old man who was so strong he could overcome a policeman; the count is nearing his century mark when he must die like other men unless he can secure the blood of a virgin to revivify him. I am more than certain that the count and baron are one and the same and that they both dwell at Rupleysville. *Voilà*, we go to Rupleysville, and we arrive there not one little minute too soon. *N'est-ce-pas, mes amis?*'

'Sure,' Costello agreed, rising and holding out his hand in farewell, 'you've got th' goods, doc. No mistake about it.'

To me, as I helped him with his coat in the hall, the detective confided, 'An' he only had one shot o' licker all evenin'! Gosh, doc, if one drink could fix me up like that I wouldn't care how much prohibition we had!'

THE MAN WHO CAST NO SHADOW